THE FIRE ESCAPE STORIES

(Volume I)

Chuck C

The Fire Escape Stories
by
Chuck Cascio

(VOLUME I—Episodes 1-9)

Bianca Rosa Publishing
Reston, VA

Trade Paperback ISBN: 1530123798
Ebook Edition ISBN13: 9781530123797

Author's Website:
Chuckcascioauthor.com

Library of Congress Control Number: 2016902953
CreateSpace Independent Publishing Platform
North Charleston, South Carolina

DEDICATION

Per Faye e la Famiglia!

The Fire Escape Stories
by
Chuck Cascio
(VOLUME I—Episodes 1-9)

CONTENTS

EPISODE #1 (PROLOGUE)

DEATH AND LIFE

Throughout my childhood, my parents, my Uncle Sal, and other family members hinted and whispered so many times about what happened to my Aunt Maria that I never asked them to reconstruct the scene in detail for me. Any discussion about her was difficult for them—I could tell that from the misty-eyed looks they shared followed by their quick headshakes and nods that were code for saying, "Not around the children." So I have constructed my own picture, really more a mass of fragmented images, of what occurred at the Brooklyn Hospital Center the morning Sally-Boy Boccanera and I were born to the DeRosa sisters on that April day in 1948:

First, I see the culmination of the emotionally surprising pregnancies, as both sisters give birth to boys of nearly identical size and weight within one minute of each other. Salvatore "Sally-Boy" Boccanera emerges first, crying, rubbing his fist-clenched hands over his eyes, and then there I am, Michael Burns, arriving rather quietly by all accounts, emitting an occasional whimper, looking a bit confused. Quickly, laughter and cheers erupt among the doctors and nurses in the room, and the two sisters reach across their beds to squeeze hands with one another while their husbands—my Uncle, Big Sal Boccanera, and my Dad, Kevin Burns—are allowed to enter the room, cheering and embracing and making the sign of the cross.

Suddenly, amid the celebratory noise, Maria DeRosa Boccanera, Sally-Boy's mother, starts to gasp for breath while holding her infant son, sounds mistaken at first for extensions of her joy, but soon her face changes to a deep red. She gags as the unseen terror of an embolism speeds like a runaway subway train into her lungs and surges into her brain. The nurses and doctors, stunned and confused at first, start to run in and out of the room, screaming orders while my own mother, Anna DeRosa Burns, holds me and stares at the scene, crying desperately. She helplessly watches her sister's eyes widen in rising fear and horror as Maria chokes and panics. Uncle Sal screams in a mixture of Italian and English, tears streaming down the stubble on his tough-guy face. He grabs at his newborn son, reaches for his wife, embraces her, begs the doctors to do more.

Then my own father, the stoic, solid, Irish Kevin Burns, reaches an arm around Big Sal in an attempt to calm him and everyone else, to figure out a solution, to determine a logical, rational way to save Aunt Maria's life.

But despite the doctors' efforts, the pleas to God, and my father's firm commitment to logic, Aunt Maria died in the bed where she had given birth to her only child. And though Big Sal lived, I could always see, or imagine I saw once I was old enough to piece together my version of Aunt Maria's death, a hole as big as his heart and a sadness that lingered behind his black eyes and pulled at his dark, square jaw. And though Sally-Boy lived and we grew together like twins, sharing our lives for many youthful years as though we were one person, I believe now that Sally-Boy reacted to an existence filled with an emptiness that he struggled mightily to understand.

You learn things along the way as you grow—at first, you just sense that things are different, and then you absorb the good times and the bad and swirl them together in your imagination, and you establish your own way of dealing with them. And, I suspect, at the very beginning, you start a cycle of questioning, answering, and adapting… though that cycle does not always provide complete answers. Sometimes a face, or a series of words or images or events, or a place, or all of these help pull things together, or as close to together as they can come.

For me, for Sally-Boy, for one another, *we* were those faces and *we* provided for one another the words and *we* shared the images and events…but for us, more than anything, there was one place that held our lives together—the gritty fire escape that jutted out from the seventh floor of the deteriorating apartment building in the Brooklyn projects where he and Uncle Sal lived. That rusty iron structure reeked in the rain, blistered in the sun, and iced over in the snow, but it was where Sally-Boy and I talked and thought and grew and philosophized and plotted and tried to understand all we could of ourselves, of one another, of our worlds, of *the* world.

But how much do we ultimately understand? Not much, really. Or a lot, perhaps. How do we measure? At some level inside ourselves, Sally-Boy and I both knew that the fire escape had special significance for each of us. But as Sally said one spring day as we sat on the warm metal floor, sharing a Pabst he had stolen from his father's refrigerator, "They call this a goddam fire escape, Mikey, but if you was tryin to escape a fire, you'd have to climb down, like, six more of these in order to get to the goddam street. All them idiots down below us would be fighting to get down, too. Fire would eat you up by then, cuz. Burned. Toast. Gone. It might rescue somebody, but it ain't gonna rescue everybody. It's not really an escape. It's just a place to go before you disappear."

That was one day before we turned seventeen.

The next day, Sally-Boy Boccanera vanished.

EPISODE #2
BLOCKS

The first time I was allowed to sit alone with Sally-Boy on the rusty fire escape outside of his father's small Brooklyn apartment, we were seven years old. I had been on it many times before, but adults had always been there with me and Sally. Still, even on those days and nights as the adults talked and smoked, for me and Sally-Boy every visit to the fire escape was filled with wrestling matches, or the two of us looking across the skyline to determine who could see the "furtherest" as he always said, or talking intensely to one another about some imaginary series of images—describing firemen making dramatic rescues, or spotting airplanes soaring overhead toward impossibly far-off places like California, or creating nighttime freaks with two-heads and six-arms, creatures that we were sure crept up the fire ladders and held frighteningly evil parties as soon as we all went inside. By the time my parents allowed me to go onto the iron platform without an adult, Sally had already been permitted by Big Sal to go on his own, so Sally-Boy was waiting for me, staring intensely over the railing at the street seven stories below.

Just before I stepped out of the oversized kitchen window that led to the fire escape, my father said to me, "You know how to behave out there, right, Michael?" I had a large paper bag of wooden blocks with me so Sally-Boy and I could build things in the warm after-noon sun. The excitement of venturing outside without an adult had me chattering and laughing nervously. But my father's tone was clear, so I calmed down and said, "Yes, Daddy, yes, I will be good. I promise."

My mother looked at him and said, "Kevin, do you think..." but my father just nodded, tapped me on the head, and helped me step up. My mother looked at me with brown eyes that, as always, covered me like a warm, safe blanket, so I said to her, too, "I will be good, Mommy. I promise."

I clutched the bag of blocks and stumbled slightly as my father let me go, and I stepped through the open window and onto the flat metal floor. Until I walked alone on the fire escape, I had never noticed how it creaked whenever I took a step, nor had I felt the odd rush that the creaking now sent into my chest. I walked tentatively over to Sally-Boy and looked down at the street with him. Something like a top spun briefly behind my eyes, and then, just as suddenly as it appeared, it stopped spinning.

"Hi, Sally-Boy," I said, turning to face him as he continued to look down.

"Hi, Mikey," he replied, not looking at me.

"Watcha lookin at?" I asked

"Street," he said.

"Why you lookin at the street?"

"I just like it. I like to see where it goes." He shrugged. Then he reached out sideways and punched me in the chest, our standard greeting, and I punched him back. We smiled simultaneously.

"Look, I have blocks," I said, holding up the bag with both hands. "Let's build something, okay?"

"Okay," Sally said, turning toward me.

We sat, and I dumped the wooden blocks onto the fire escape floor. They clanged loudly, and I saw my mother peering cautiously at me from inside the apartment. She blew me a kiss and then turned away after I waved to her.

"What do you want to make?" I asked.

"I don't care," Sally said. "Let's just build. Let's see."

I started moving the larger blocks to make a foundation, while Sally-Boy took the smaller pieces aside and began making a series of oddly shaped structures. After several minutes of working separately, Sally suddenly stopped and said, "Smell that?"

"Yeah, pew! Did you…"

"No, it's from down there," he said, pointing toward a factory at the end of the block. "It's where they make the beer. Stinky."

"I didn't know beer was smelly. I never smelled it before ever."

"Papa says it's just smelly when they make it. Not when they drink it." He picked up one of the strange looking objects he had constructed. It looked roughly like a windmill, and he pointed it at the factory. "I can make the smell go away," he said. He stood with it and held it on the fire escape railing. "Go away, stinky beer stink! This fan makes you go away!"

I stood up next to him and called out, "Beer stinks! Go away!"

We started waving our hands, Sally-Boy still holding the wooden fan, when Big Sal stuck his head out of the window and called to us: "What are you knuckleheads doin? Don't you throw nothin off that fire escape, you hear? You throw somethin off that fire escape, and you are gonna get the '*te-te*.' Sally-Boy knows the '*te-te*.' You know the '*te-te*' too, right, Mikey?" Big Sal moved his hand sideways in a slicing motion, Italian slang for spanking.

"Yes, Uncle Sal. I do. We are being good. We aren't throwing anything, I promise."

"Sally-Boy? You throwin anything?'

"No, Papa. Just wavin away the beer stink."

"Oh, okay," Big Sal said, as he moved his head back inside the apartment, "if that is what you are doin, that is good. Get rid of that stink! But you throw anythin, you get the *te-te*!" He sliced the air with his palm again and pretended to bite the end of it for added emphasis.

My mother waved to us from behind my Uncle Sal. "Your Momma is nice," Sally-Boy said.

"Yeah. She makes real good pasta, too," I said.

"I don't have a Momma," Sally-Boy said. "She died."

"I know," I said. "She and my Mom were sisters."

"Yeah, I know that. I don't know why my Momma had to die."

"Well…she's in heaven," I said with conviction.

"Yeah, I guess." Sally-Boy looked at me, his lips expressing either slight sadness or emerging trouble. "She's not at the other place, the other one that begins with H."

I shook my head. "Don't say that word, Sally! It's bad."

Sally-Boy punched me and sat back down. I followed him to the warm floor. He looked at the strong, solid base I had built with my blocks.

"Watch this," he said.

One-by-one, Sally took the structures that seemed to have sprung randomly from his head and placed them carefully on the base of blocks I had created. "I can make them stand," Sally said. "Watch. Every one of them."

"Well, some might fall down maybe, Sally, but if they do, I will help you put them back like they were. Okay? I will help you."

Sally stopped and looked at me, pushing his face and shoulders forward slightly. "Well, if they fall, they don't really ever get put all back together again 'cause then they're just in pieces and they stay in pieces."

"But," I started to say, and as I did, Sally took one small block and casually threw it over his shoulder, over the railing, and toward the street below.

"Whoops, it slipped!" he said, laughing.

I looked at him in horror at first and then quickly scanned the apartment window, certain that Big Sal or my father or mother had seen what Sally had done and would rush out to get us. But no one had seen and nothing happened, and then Sally went ahead and started placing his wooden structures on top of the base I had built. As he did so, I stood and leaned against the top rail of the fire escape and looked down the street toward the beer factory. The odor seemed to have dissipated, but thick gray smoke billowed like grotesquely shaped shadows escaping from its smokestacks.

"Done it!" Sally-Boy announced.

I turned to see his strange creations placed solidly on my wooden base.

Sally-Boy stood. "None of them fell down," he said proudly.

"Nope," I said, squatting to look closely at his unusual constructions. "They look real good, Sally!"

Just then, my father tapped at the window and motioned that it was time for me to come inside, time to go home to our brownstone a few blocks away. I waved to him.

"I have to take the blocks," I said to Sally.

"Let's leave 'em."

"But I gotta go home."

"But if you take them, then they will be in pieces."

"But I will bring them back, and we will make something new next time."

With that, Sally grabbed a random handful of blocks, jumped up, and threw them over the fire escape in the direction of the beer factory.

"Beer stinks!" he yelled, laughing.

"Why'd you do that, Sally!"

"Fun," he said calmly. "They fly down, but you can't tell where they land."

"My blocks, Sally! Those were mine!"

"Throw one," he said, handing me a short, oblong piece. "Watch it the furtherest way down as you can."

"I'll get in trouble," I said, but I took the small block from his hand.

"Drop it. It's just a block. It's fun to watch."

I leaned over the black railing and held out the block. I turned to look at Sally. He just nodded and said again, "Drop it."

I let the block go and watched it fall as far as I could, but from seven stories high, I could not see it land. Still, my chest filled with a strange, unfamiliar heat and questions spun in my head about what falling felt like and whether I would ever find the blocks and if I would get in trouble. I looked back at Sally. He was laughing. I could see my parents and Uncle Sal talking inside the apartment; they had not seen what I had done.

"I'm pickin up the rest of them," I said to Sally-Boy as I dismantled the structures and put the blocks in the bag.

"They're all in pieces again," he said, watching me, but not helping.

"We can build something different next time," I said.

"And we can throw more over the fire escape," he said, laughing.

I looked at him and tried to stifle a laugh of my own. "Maybe," I said.

Then he opened his hand to reveal one more piece. Casually, again without looking, he flipped it high in the air and over the railing. He imitated the shocked look on my face as together we watched the block shrink as it fell.

"Funny, huh?" he said, looking down.

I was silent for a moment. I considered his question and squinted as I followed the free-falling block as far as

I could. "Yeah, kinda," I said, "but we don't really get to see where any of them land."

Sally shook his head. "Nope. Who cares?" he said, and then he quickly grabbed the railing, leaned over it, and spat in the direction of the beer factory.

EPISODE #3

CANNOLI E FRATELLI

Panificio di Boccanera was the most popular bakery in all of Brooklyn, its awning covering three rickety wooden tables on the sidewalk, its neon sign glowing over a sketch of the Amalfi Coast, an Italian flag proudly on display in the lone front window, and opera music echoing nonstop from a small phonograph inside. Big Sal owned *Panificio,* and it was his personal connection to his parents, who had established their own small bakery in the city of Amalfi. At age twelve, Big Sal's parents had sent him out of Italy with his aunt and uncle to the States just in time for him to experience the Great Depression, while living with a huge family of relatives in a cramped Brooklyn apartment. Big Sal never saw his parents nor his brother and sister again.

"I always said I was gonna go back, but I never made it," Uncle Sal would often tell people at *Panificio,* where everyone seemed to become instant friends. "Still, someday, I'm gonna get back there. Maria and I said we would go as soon our first kid was born, but, well…" His voice would fade, but then he would sweep his hands around the bakery, point to a picture of Aunt Maria, and say, "That is my Maria, and this, this is my *Panificio di Boccanera,* and this is how I honor *mi famiglia*! Just like my Papa's place in Amalfi, that's what I have here."

He had borrowed money shortly after World War II to open the shop. Of course, the men he borrowed from made certain permanent demands of him—he paid the men regularly, though they performed no service. They ate whatever they wanted for free and could sip espresso and cappuccino all day. Sometimes they would close the bakery on a moment's notice, telling any customers that it was time for them to leave. The men would turn off the neon light, put out a "closed" sign, draw all the shades, and engage in discussions no one dared ask about. But the *Panificio di Boccanera* was, as the New York *Daily News* called it in a review, "The most authentic Italian bakery in all of Brooklyn…like sipping the most delicious coffee and nibbling on the freshest cannoli in Amalfi with your *fratelli e sorelle.* And the owner, Big Sal Boccanera, is always there to greet everyone who stops in."

The other families in the Brooklyn apartment building where Uncle Sal lived all helped him out at home by taking care of the infant Sally-Boy, but when Sally-Boy turned three years old, Big Sal started bringing him to the bakery every day. Sally quickly became an added attraction with his unique stare and sudden outbursts of questions. People would stop in just to chat with the little boy behind the counter who would pretend to write down their orders for the bakery's homemade brutti-boni, tartufo, tiramisu, gelato, or any number of other items. And little Sally would try hard to belt out what he determined were the lyrics to an aria from *La Boheme* or *Madama Butterfly*.

Big Sal and Sally-Boy welcomed everyone to their little slice of Italy, Sally-Boy growing and eventually serving coffee and sweets at the counter or at the six small wooden tables inside the store. When Sally and I reached school age, I started to help out at the bakery every afternoon, while my parents were at work. Sally and I took orders, cleaned tables, and handed coffee to the people standing along the walls. I was often called "Sally-Boy" and he was called "Mikey," since we were the same size and looked so much alike with our thick black hair, though my eyes were brown and Sally's were black.

But shortly after Sally-Boy and I turned eight years old, something started to change. He and I were walking to the bakery after St. Anne's Elementary School dismissed one day, when Sally said, shaking his head, "I don't wanna go to the bakery today." He stopped walking, looking around suspiciously, as though he expected something or someone to step out of one of the cars on the street or to emerge from the nearby subway stop.

"What? Why? Why shouldn't we go to the bakery today?" I asked.

Sally looked at the sky where a helicopter churned rhythmically overhead. "Boring," he said. "And the people pinch me and you, and they make jokes all the time. And they want me to sing the stupid opera. Besides, Papa makes us work too hard."

Big Sal's demands of us had never seemed particularly outrageous to me. Move some tubs of sprinkles around (we always grabbed several handfuls and shoved them into our mouths), throw the trash, serve the customers, clean the counters and the glass display case. Plus, I enjoyed the loud talk in the bakery about baseball, which made me imagine playing for the Dodgers before the team left all of Brooklyn forlorn and angry, and the cursing about politics, which I didn't understand, and apparently—based on the amount of laughter—lots of dirty jokes told in Italian, which I also didn't understand…though I tried mightily to do so.

"It's sorta fun there, Sally. Come on. Your Papa's gonna wonder where we are. And he's gonna be mad. So will my parents be mad. We will get in trouble."

But Sally-Boy was already walking in the opposite direction, while watching the helicopter become just a speck among white clouds. "You go!" he said excitedly. "Make believe I had to stay after school to help Sister Emma Loretta, but not because I was bad."

"But that's a lie!" I shouted as he moved farther away. "Your Papa, he will be so mad when he finds out."

"It will be okay," Sally shouted back. "We don't lie so much!"

Then he ran up the street and disappeared around the corner, and I stood there in the sunlight wondering what to do. "Sally!" I yelled. "Sally! Come back here! Sallyyyyy!"

An elderly woman stuck her head out of her apartment window and called down to me: "Whatsamatta wit you, little boy? You need some help or somethin'? All that yellin'! Make-a shut-up, eh? Ooofa!"

I looked up at her. "But," I stammered, "but he ran away!" She was partially covered by the clothes drying on a tight rope line that stretched across her fire escape.

"Who? Who run away that you yell like this? You friend? He run away?"

"No, no, it was him, it was Sally-Boy, my…my brother."

"So tell-a you Momma, but you stop-a the damn yellin now! Go, go tell-a you Momma! But now, you make-a the shut-up, eh!" She slammed down the window.

When I arrived at the bakery without Sally-Boy, Uncle Sal handed me my usual after-school cannoli and immediately asked where Sally-Boy was.

"He stayed after school," I blurted out quickly, "but not because he was bad, Uncle Sal. He wasn't bad. He was just helping Sister Emma Loretta. That's all. He wasn't bad." I was unable to take even a small bite of the cannoli.

"Come on now, Mikey," Uncle Sal said quietly. "Did Sally-Boy do somethin wrong?"

"No, no he didn't, Uncle Sal, he just…he just wanted to help Sister…" and then I started to choke back tears.

Uncle Sal hugged me. "It's okay, Mikey. I will find out what's goin on. You sit down. You eat your cannoli. Don't you worry about it. You're a good boy, Mikey."

"I don't feel like eating right now," I said.

"Then you save it for later, Mikey. That's fine." Uncle Sal turned to the young Italian couple who helped him in the shop, Massimo Bortuzzi and his wife Angelina, who had been listening. "Watch Mikey for me, will ya? His Momma will be by to pick him up at the usual time. I gotta go find Sally-Boy."

They nodded. Uncle Sal yanked off his apron, walked through the small crowd in the bakery, but without shaking hands or laughing as he usually did, and then quickly started running up the street.

Even at age eight, I knew that Angelina Bortuzzi was beautiful, and when she came over and hugged me, I felt strange. "You no worry about Sally-Boy, Mikey," she said in her broken English. "He's a-gonna be good, eh? Here, you eat a little of the cannoli and you will feel better, okay? You do for me, for Angelina. I will even eat some with you." She took a small bite. "*Delizioso*! Here, for you."

I nibbled at the piece of cannoli she had broken off and held in her hand. "There you go," Angelina said. "The cannoli, it helps to make everything better, no?"

I nodded and ate some more. Then I said, "Sally-Boy's coming back, right, Angelina?"

She hugged me and said, "Yes, yes, now you no worry, Michael. I go to help Massimo now. Look how crowded the shop is getting! But Salvatore, he's a-comin back."

She smiled at me, and my eyes involuntarily flicked down at the floor. As she started to walk away, I said, "Angelina?"

"Yes, Michael?"

"Can I have another cannoli?"

"But you no finish this cannoli...and I no think-a you parents want that you have more than one of the cannoli, eh, do you?"

"It's not for me, Angelina."

"Oh? Who you will give it to? You girlfriend-a?" she teased. "Handsome guy like you must have the girl-friend-a who like the cannoli, no?"

My face flushed, and I shook my head vigorously. "No, no, I don't have a girlfriend, Angelina. I don't like girls. It's, it's for Sally-Boy."

She handed me another cannoli and focused her brown eyes, which seemed to expand like brown balloons, directly into mine. "You know where is Salvatore?" she asked.

"No, no, not right now. But I know where he will be."

"Oh? You do? Where is this?"

"On the fire escape. And he will be hungry."

Angelina rubbed a hand through my black curls and then wrapped the cannoli for Sally-Boy. "You are a good *cugino*, Michael, the best cousin. You should always help take care of Salvatore, and he will take care of you, too. Here's a cannoli you give your *cugino*, Salvatore, later."

"Actually," I said, "we're brothers." I took another bite of my cannoli, put Sally's in a paper bag, and quickly headed toward the front door of the bakery.

"Ah, the *fratelli*, you and Salvatore, eh, the brothers?" she said warmly, moving her hands to her chest.

I nodded and started out the front door.

"Wait! Come back here, Michael!" Angelina called. "I say for you should give it to Salvatore later, no now!"

But I was already running down the block. Three blocks away I was at Sally-Boy's apartment, and then, after running up seven flights of stairs, I knocked on Sally-Boy's door, hoping he might be hiding inside. When no one answered, I used my key to get in. The apartment was empty, and so was the fire escape off the kitchen. I opened the large window, climbed onto the fire escape, and placed the bag with the cannoli in it in a corner.

As I started to climb back into the apartment, I heard a noise in the sky, and I looked up to see a helicopter approaching, growing louder and larger by the second, and I wondered if it could be the same one Sally-Boy had been looking at earlier. Then, for a moment, as the engine's noise grew louder like an approaching thunderstorm and the copter itself seemed to quickly expand in size, I thought it might actually hit the tenement building. Frightened, I grabbed ahold of the fire escape railing, closed my eyes, and clung tightly to our safe space. But the chopper flew safely overhead, its once rhythmic engine sounding briefly like random explosions. I opened my eyes to see it absorbed into the clouds, the sound of its engine lingering even as the copter itself disappeared. Then, for some reason, I started to talk out loud and eventually started singing in a semi-operatic voice into the empty air off the fire escape, "There's a cannoli waiting for yooouuuu, Sally-Booooy! Come and get it, Salvatoreeeee! The cannoli is yoooours, Sally-Boooy, so come home now and geeeeet iiiiit, Sally-Boooy..."

I ran back down the stairs, out the front door, and back to the bakery, where Angelina was waiting for me in the doorway. She looked more sad than angry.

"You make-a me scare, Michael!" she said. "Please, promise you no do that again. You and Salvatore should no run away."

"I'm sorry, Angelina, I promise," I said, looking down at my sneakers.

She hugged me. "Okay, you are good boy. Now come…you help Angelina clean the counters, eh?"

"Okay."

Massimo saw us enter, and he called out from behind the display case, "You and your *cugino* gotta cut it out! Yous both causing the troubles today, Michael!"

Angelina squeezed my shoulder and said to Massimo, "They're not the *cugini*, Mass. They are the *fratelli*—the brothers—eh, Michael?"

I nodded.

"Okay," Massimo said with a shrug. He threw me a damp cloth, which I caught. "Good catch," he said. "Now, you know what to do with it, so go do it, eh? You 'brother,' he's no here to help you, so you gotta do it all youself. "

I immediately began cleaning the counters and the glass cases filled with baked goods.

"You give the cannoli to Salvatore, Michael?" Angelina asked.

I stopped cleaning, looked directly at Angelina, and said in a shaky voice, "No, Angelina. I just put it on the fire escape. Sally, he's gonna sit on that fire escape and eat that cannoli. He's gonna eat that cannoli right there. I just know it."

"Yes, Michael, I know it, too," she said. She leaned over and kissed me on the top of my head, and I hid my face in her apron. "Sally-Boy, he gonna be fine, Michael. You take the good care of him."

"I did take care of him, right, Angelina?" I asked, barely able to speak into her apron.

"Yes, Michael, yes, you did."

A short while later, I was sitting in a corner of the bakery, working on homework, when Uncle Sal walked in with Sally-Boy next to him. Uncle Sal shook hands and chatted in Italian with the customers as he entered. Sally was smiling. They both walked over to me, and Uncle Sal grabbed my head and rubbed it with his knuckles. "You kids," he said, "you gonna make us all crazy."

Angelina hugged Sally-Boy, and Massimo stood there shaking his head, a hint of a smile beneath his mustache.

"Where did you go, Sally?" I asked.

He turned away from Angelina and faced me. "Played some stickball, walked around, saw some other neighborhoods, went home. That's all."

Angelina held Sally-Boy by the back of his shoulders. "You got the cannoli, eh?"

"Yes," Sally said, looking straight at me.

"And you know who left it for you, the cannoli, eh?" Angelina asked.

"Yes," Sally said, pulling up a chair next to me, and elbowing me gently in the side. "He did. Mikey left it for me."

"*Fratelli*," Angelina said, her eyes glistening with warmth. "Salvatore, you know what this means, *fratelli*?"

"Brothers," he said, as I elbowed him back. "It means brothers."

EPISODE #4

SQUEAKS

Sister Emma Loretta had an announcement to make, so she smashed her yardstick against her desk repeatedly, despite the fact that the entire fourth-grade class at St. Anne's Elementary already sat at perfect attention, hands folded, looking at the crucifix above Sister's head. When she finally stopped, she looked around the room in absolute silence for what seemed like an hour. Then she said to me, "Why do you think I have to do that to get everyone's attention, Michael?"

"I don't know, Sister," I said, looking straight ahead at her, fearful that my gaze might slip, or I might blink.

"I asked, 'Why do you *think* I have to do that,' Michael?" she said, not changing inflection except for adding emphasis to the one word. She stared directly into my eyes. "You can *think*, can't you?"

"Yes, Sister," I said.

"Well, if you can *think*, then you can tell me what you *think* made me do that, Michael, can't you?"

"Yes, Sister. Maybe someone was not sitting up straight, Sister, or maybe someone did not have their hands folded, Sister."

"Is that what you *think*, Michael?"

"Yes, Sister."

"Well, Michael, you are never completely correct, and you are not completely correct this time either. But you are at least *partially* correct for a change." She lifted her eyes from mine and faced the entire class. "Someone was not sitting straight, someone else allowed their eyes to drift from looking at our Lord, Jesus Christ, on the cross, and someone else did not keep their hands folded. So there will be punishment! You will all go to recess now, but on the playground, there will be no talking, no noise, no sounds from you! If you must play, you will play in silence, and even as you play, you will use it as meditation time...time to think about your sins and why you are all incapable of being fully obedient! Do you all understand?"

In unison, the class responded, "Yes, Sister!" Sister Emma barked orders, and we stood and lined up, military style, at the doorway. She walked down the line, nodding, and then said, "Go then, children. You have twenty minutes of Silent Recess during which you can meditate as you play your games and pray and thank the Lord for all you have. Maybe, *perhaps*, then you will understand that the games you play...," then she paused before, whispering, but loud enough for us all to hear, "... have been made available to you through the *Lord's* will!"

Just as she finished that pronouncement, Sally-Boy, who was standing directly behind me, let out a barely audible "squeak," as though a mouse had suddenly decided to make a single, subtle statement about something ridiculous. I somehow forced myself to refrain from laughing, nearly choking in the process, knowing that if I so much as hinted at a smile, Sister would pounce on me with nearly boundless fury.

In the cool spring air, thirty fourth grade boys and girls—separated, of course, by a bright yellow line with the words "Boys" on one side and "Girls" on the other—moved around the concrete playground in utter silence. Eventually, a game of tag broke out on the boys' side, while the girls had several lines of silent jump rope going. Sister Emma patrolled the playground to make sure there was no talking, though she occasionally broke the silence by saying, "Think about Jesus, children, who died for your sins for without his gift, you would have no games to play!"

The rhythmic thump of the jump ropes contrasted greatly with the silently chaotic game of tag that had developed as boys ran around randomly tagging one another in animated silence and pretending to stomp their feet if they thought they had been tagged unfairly, which is exactly what every boy thought.

Toward the end of the twenty-minute recess, Billy O'Dell, the smallest boy in the class, put both hands up to signal that he no longer wanted to play the increasingly frenetic game of silent tag. He leaned against the schoolyard fence, breathing hard and wheezing, as he often did whenever he had run for even a minute or two. Sister Emma Loretta blew her whistle once, signaling that we had just one more minute of recess left, and Billy started to move slowly away from the fence. As he did so, Monty Grafenski, the biggest boy in the class, snuck up behind him and kicked Billy, sending him sprawling onto the cold concrete. Sally-Boy and I were walking behind them, Sally providing an occasional squeak just to see if he could get me to laugh out loud. But when Sally saw Monty kick Billy, he shouted, "Hey! Why did you do that, Monty?"

Immediately, from the opposite end of the small schoolyard, Sister Emma Loretta's whistle pierced the air like a shrill scream, and she shouted, "Who is yelling? Who is violating the rules? Was that you, Salvatore?"

"It was Salvatore, Sister!" Monty called out, "Salvatore kicked Billy so hard that poor Billy fell down!"

Billy O'Dell had not seen who kicked him, and as he got up from the ground and brushed at his scraped school pants, he had tears in his eyes. "Why did you do that, Sally?" he asked. "I thought…I thought you and Mikey was my friends."

"We are your friends, Billy; it was Monty who did it," Sally said, and I added, "Yeah, Billy, it was Monty, not Sally who kicked you."

Just then, Sister Emma Loretta rushed up behind us, the long string of thick rosary beads at her side clacking loudly, and she grabbed Sally by the back of his jacket and started shaking him. Sally's jacket, shirt, and tie bunched up tightly against his neck as Sister shook him, his arms dangling helplessly out of control. "You have violated the Lord's playground, Salvatore!" Sister shouted. Sally's face flushed, yet he somehow remained calm. "You have violated the rules of a Sister of the Lord! You have ruined the holy meditation of two of your classmates! You will be punished here at school, Salvatore, and in the afterlife!"

As she shook Sally, Monty Grafenski smiled quickly, and when I saw that, I clenched both of my fists at my side. Monty saw my gesture and simply rolled his eyes. By now, all the other kids on the playground had gathered, still in silence, around Sister Emma Loretta, who barked to everyone as she continued to shake Sally-Boy, "All of you get in two lines—boys in one, girls in the other! Do not look at one another! Do not do anything other than pray!"

Sister dragged Sally to the Mother Superior's office, and he never returned to the classroom that day. After school, Monty Grafenski walked up next to me as I tried to locate Sally and said, "You want me to punch you, Michael? I will. I can punch anyone I want."

"You lied today, Monty," I said, "and that got Sally in trouble."

"'*Sally*' is a girl's name, dummy," he said. "You sound like a girl when you talk about him. You probably punch like a little girl, like Gina Falengina would punch. I know how to punch. I can punch anyone I want." He balled his fist and held it an inch in front of my nose.

Just then, Sally emerged from Mother Superior's office. Uncle Sal was with him. "Come on, Mikey," Uncle Sal said. "We gotta go. Sally won't be goin to school with you tomorrow."

"You been kicked out?" I asked.

Sally nodded. "For one day," he said. "But I can't do recess for a month."

"But you didn't do anything," I said. I turned to Big Sal, who was shaking his head as he looked at Sally Boy. "Uncle Sal, Sally was just trying to help Billy because Billy got kicked by Monty. Sally was trying to help him, Uncle Sal. It's not fair."

"Well, that's not what the Sister says, Mikey, and I got no time to argue. Gotta get back to the bakery. Think you two can go to the apartment, change clothes, and then get to the bakery without gettin in no more trouble?"

Sally and I nodded in unison.

Big Sal walked in one direction toward his bakery, and we walked in the other toward Sally-Boy's apartment. Sally was quiet during the entire five-block walk. When I asked questions like, "What did Mother Superior say to you? Did you tell her it was Monty? Why does Monty think he can punch whoever he wants?" he just looked straight ahead, his eyes focused on something I could not see.

When we got to the apartment, we changed out of our school clothes, and Sally-Boy handed me a glass of lemonade from the refrigerator, took one for himself, and then nodded silently toward the fire escape. We climbed through the window and onto the platform, and quietly sipped our drinks. Finally, Sally said firmly, "I am going to get him."

"Who?" I asked.

"Monty. I am going to get him."

"But you won't be at school tomorrow," I said. "Besides, you'll get in more trouble."

"Monty can't just kick kids or punch kids because he's big. Billy's little, and he can't fight. I can fight." Sally-Boy put the lemonade down and raised his fists to me and started flicking punches.

"I don't wanna fight you, Sally."

"I don't wanna fight you either, dopey. I'm just showin you what I can do."

I put my lemonade down and started firing punches back at him, and the next thing we knew we were shadow boxing and wrestling and laughing on the fire escape, even as we banged off of its iron railings.

As we walked toward the bakery, we passed the school. Just off the playground, a small circle of students still in their school uniforms—boys in white shirts and plain blue ties, girls in blue-and-gray checkered skirts and white blouses—cheered and laughed at something. We walked toward them and saw some of the students spinning Billy O'Dell in circles and then laughing hysterically at him as he dizzily tried to walk and pick up the contents of his book bag, which had been strewn along the ground. At the center, Monty Grafenski slapped Billy in the head every time he turned away. Suddenly, Sally ran toward the group, shouting, "Hey! Hey, stop that, Monty!" I ran quickly behind him. The circle around Billy opened up when we arrived, and when Monty spotted us, he casually tossed Billy to the ground and stood with one foot on Billy's back. Sally bent down and tried to help Billy up, but Monty pushed his foot down harder. Billy cried into the dirt.

"What do you want?" Monty asked, looking at Sally. "You already been kicked outta school." Then he turned toward me. "Do you wanna get kicked out, too?"

Sally started to say something, but an image of us shadow boxing on the fire escape flashed in my mind, and I leapt straight at Monty and shouted "Let Billy up now!" in his face. Monty seemed to smile quickly and he threw a punch at me, but I ducked it and punched him hard in the stomach. Monty made a sound like a balloon bursting; his foot lifted off of Billy, and Sally-Boy helped Billy up. I jumped on Monty, wrapping him in a head-lock. I could feel and smell his rank, heavy breath as I wrestled him to the ground. "You got Sally kicked out!" I shouted, twisting Monty's head into the dirt as hard as I could. "You lied and you got him kicked out!" Monty made a series of high-pitched noises, like a wounded bird, as he mumbled something under my grip. He kicked his legs and flailed his arms on the ground, but I squeezed tighter and tighter and the ground swallowed his incoherent mumbles. Other kids cheered, mostly for me, but some urged Monty to get up.

"Please let me up," Monty begged shrilly from under me. "Please, I give up, let me up."

I released my grip, and Monty stood slowly. He was a good head taller than I was, but the redness in his eyes and the dirt on his face and clothes made him look less intimidating. He started to brush himself off, and then he launched a sudden punch at me, shouting, "I can punch anyone I want!" But I quickly leaned back, and his swing whooshed past me. Then I landed my right fist against Monty's left eye and easily wrestled him to the ground again.

As Monty squirmed beneath me, I realized that the cheers from students had ended, and I heard Sally-Boy saying, "Let him go, Mikey, let him go, quick!" Before I could release Monty, someone grabbed the back of my shirt and shook me so hard I felt my shirt collar rip. Then I heard her voice.

"You will join your cousin in suspension tomorrow, Michael Burns!" Sister Emma Loretta hissed in my ear. "You have offended the Lord and you have harmed a fellow student! You are punished here and will be punished in the hereafter! Come with me! The rest of you sinful children, go home!"

Billy O'Dell said, "But Sister..."

"Go home, William!" she ordered. "Go home, all of you except for Michael and Salvatore!"

As Billy and the other children walked away, he looked toward me and Sally-Boy. He seemed desperate to say something, but Sally-Boy moved one hand as if he were wiping an imaginary counter at Big Sal's bakery, and Billy nodded knowingly. Monty cleaned himself off as best he could and kept touching the bruise on his cheekbone that had already begun to form, but he did not look at me or Sally. He just shuffled away, alone, still making an indecipherable noise.

Sally walked with me and Sister Emma to Mother Superior's stale-smelling office where the gray walls were filled with drawings and paintings of the Virgin Mary. Mother Superior did not say a word to me or Sally-Boy. She just took off her eyeglasses, wiped them on a piece of tissue, put them back on, and motioned for us to sit in two folding chairs in a corner. Mother Superior thumbed through a file folder, pulled out a paper, and called my mother at work in the clothing factory, where she was one of many seamstresses, to tell her I could not come to school the next day. She handed me the phone, and my mother said, "We will talk about this at home, Michael, okay?"

"Yes, Mom. I'm sorry, Mom."

"Okay, now you go to the bakery with Sally-Boy, and Daddy or I will pick you up there at the usual time."

"Okay," I said.

I handed the phone back to Mother Superior, who took it and simply said, "Go."

Sally and I left her office and walked quietly toward Big Sal's bakery. Suddenly, without looking at me, Sally-Boy started squeaking, quietly at first, but then getting louder and louder.

"What are you doing?" I asked, starting to laugh.

"Did you hear Monty when you had him on the ground? He sounded like he was a squeaker."

"Yeah," I said, imitating, as best I could, the sound I had heard Monty making.

Soon Sally and I were walking along the Brooklyn streets, laughing and punching playfully at one another, shouting randomly in high-pitched voices: "'Squeak squeak...I am big tough Monty! Squeak! Squeak! I can punch whoever I want! Squeak squeak! Let me up off the ground! Squeak squeak! Looks like we'll be spending tomorrow at the bakery! Squeak squeak! We hate school! Squeak squeak!"

We were still laughing and squeaking when we walked into the bustling bakery that afternoon. People sipping their coffees and nibbling their pastries caught the contagious laughter and nonsensical sounds of two young boys, and soon the bakery was filled with laughter and squeaking customers who grabbed us playfully, shouting things like, "Whatsa matta wit yous? You makin it crazy in here wit the squeaks! Hahahaha! I make the squeaks, too, eh, like the Squeaky Boys! Squeak! Squeak! Squeak!"

Massimo Bortuzzi looked at Big Sal and said, "*A pazzo a pazzo!*" pointing to his head and shouting through the noise. Angelina laughed loudly and squeaked wildly with us.

Uncle Sal just shook his head, hugging Sally and I as we squeaked, and said as he swept his arm around the squeaking, laughing patrons of *Panificio di Boccanera*, "*Si, a pazzo*, Massimo—these boys, they make such craziness. But, hey, they make such happiness, too, these knuckleheads, they make the happiness, too."

EPISODE #5

THE DELIVERY MEN

The first morning of summer vacation after Sally-Boy and I had finished fifth grade, we were in the bakery at 5 AM. Uncle Sal had said there was a "business arrangement" he wanted to discuss with us, and he needed us both there an hour before the shop opened. The aroma of freshly baking pastries filled the air like an invisible, delicious feast. I had been awake most of the night, wondering what Uncle Sal was going to ask us to do. Despite my persistent questioning the night before, my parents professed no knowledge of his plans:

"Do you think he'll teach us how to bake?" I asked, imagining myself working in the kitchen next to Angelina Bortuzzi, following her instructions for making Italian delicacies...and, yes, simultaneously sneaking peeks at her.

"You'll just have to wait and see, Mikey," my mother said. "You know Uncle Sal. He is always full of surprises."

"Big Sal will probably have you mopping up that restroom," my father said in his typically flat tone. "That wouldn't be so bad. Maybe then you and your goombah, Sally-Boy, can think about some of the trouble you caused during the school year and see where you wind up when you do that kind of stuff."

"Sorry, Dad," I said, but then blurted, "but do you really think that's what Uncle Sal wants us to do? Clean the bathroom?"

My father emitted a quick chuckle from behind the New York *Post* he was reading, and my mother said, "No, Mikey, I am sure Uncle Sal will have something better for you boys. You're both getting so big now, and your Uncle and your Dad both know that you did well in school this year." She turned to my father and said, "Isn't that right, Kevin? I mean, after all, Mikey made the honor roll."

My father peered from behind the paper and let his version of a smile slide to the right of his lips. "Yeah, I guess so, Anna. Michael did okay. Salvatore...well, I don't know..."

"Sally-Boy passed, Kevin," she interrupted, "so I am sure Big Sal has something special planned for the boys."

"Yeah," my father said, his lips still slightly at an angle, "maybe it will keep them out of trouble and, who knows, they might just learn something useful."

So I stood with Sally-Boy in the bakery, the morning sun struggling to break through a slight drizzle that fogged over the tenements across from the bakery. As usual, Sally and I were punching and elbowing one another playfully, when Uncle Sal peeked out of the kitchen and called to us. "Come here, you guys," he said. "Time to quit the foolin around and talk business...like real men."

Angelina and Massimo stood next to Uncle Sal and greeted us as we entered. *"Buon giorno,"* Angelina said warmly. Massimo simply pushed his square jaw upward and tilted his head back slightly, his personal form of greeting.

Uncle Sal said, "Angelina, Massimo, you know these *testa dura, si?"*

Angelina said, "Of course, Big Sal, but they are not the 'hard heads!' They are the good boys, the brothers."

"Testa dura fratelli," Massimo joked.

Uncle Sal laughed and said, "Well, the 'Hard Head Brothers' are gonna be workin with you two this summer."

Sally-Boy and I exchanged a quick, excited glance, since we had talked many times in code about the various virtues of Angelina. The thought of working in proximity with her immediately captured our growing imaginations.

"What will we do, Uncle Sal?" I asked, trying to control my excitement.

"Well," he said, "you two are gonna be our delivery men. This summer, me and Massimo and Angelina are takin orders from people who live within five blocks of the bakery. Then you knuckleheads are gonna deliver their orders to them by eight o'clock in the morning— no later. So yous gotta be here no later than six, have your good sneakers on, each of you bring a wagon, load the goods onto the wagons, get the list of addresses from Massimo and Angelina, and get the stuff delivered on time. *Capisci?*"

"Yes, Uncle Sal, I understand."

"Me too, Papa," Sally-Boy said, "but…"

"Yeah, Salvatore, but what?" Uncle Sal raised his eyebrows and smiled at his son.

"Well, you know, Papa," Sally-Boy said, "that's a lot of work, and I was wonderin…"

"Spit it out, Salvatore," Uncle Sal said. "This is what they call 'negotiatin.'"

"Are we gonna get paid, Papa?" Sally finally blurted out.

"Oh, oofa!" Massimo shouted with a laugh, waving his muscular arms at us like he was brushing aside a foul smell. "These kids, look at them! They want the money."

"No, it's…" I started to say, because I really hadn't even considered that we would get paid, but Uncle Sal cut me off.

He turned to Massimo and Angelina and said, "What do you think, Mass? Angelina? Should I pay these *vermi*, eh?" Massimo motioned for all three of them to get together, and they all mumbled in Italian, waved their arms, and rolled their eyes as though they were in deep, contentious discussion.

Finally, they turned to face us and Uncle Sal said, "Here's what has been decided. You each get half a dollar per day as long as all the goods are delivered by eight o'clock every morning. You don't deliver by eight, you get *niente. Capisci?*"

"Yes, Uncle Sal, thank you," I said immediately. The prospect of making over three dollars in a week made my head spin. Sally-Boy, however, just stood there nodding.

"What is it Salvatore?" Uncle Sal asked. "You don't like the deal? You better, because it is the deal."

"Well, Papa," Sally said slowly, "I just was wondering about one more thing."

"What, Salvatore? Say it quickly because we all have work to do."

"The tips," Sally said. "What about the tips. Do we get to keep the tips?"

Uncle Sal burst into laughter and turned to Massimo and Angelina, who were smiling and shaking their heads. "What am I gonna do with this kid, eh?" Uncle Sal said. "He thinks people are gonna give them the tips!" He turned to us and said, "Sure, if yous get the tips, yous get to keep the tips. Now both of yous run home, get your wagons, and get back here within fifteen minutes—not sixteen, not seventeen—fifteen! You gotta get ready for your first deliveries this morning. Who knows? Maybe you'll get the tips today! Oh, and put on the shirts. Angelina, you have the shirts?"

"*Si*," Angelina said, pulling two tee-shirts out of a bag she was holding. She held them up; on the front, each had a picture of a cannoli with the words: *Uomini di Consegna Panificio*, and on the back was the name of the bakery. "I make-a these shirts just-a for you," she said proudly.

"What does it mean?" I asked, looking at the front of the shirt.

Before Angelina could answer, Sally-Boy translated for me: "Bakery Delivery Men."

"Very good with the *Italiano*, Salvatore!" Angelina said. Then she put the shirt on each of us, and when she did, I felt a strange vibration run through my body, and I could only stare at the floor as she, Massimo, and Uncle Sal cheered for me and Sally-Boy.

From that first delivery day, the summer developed as a sort of fantasy. Early-morning Brooklyn provided a daily set of surprises that fed my imagination as I walked to the bakery in the emerging dawn, pulling my wagon, wondering if the blasts from distant ships' horns across the water might actually be human voices calling for a new day to begin. Every morning, I said hello to an African American man sitting on an old wooden plank on a street corner. He wore a tattered World War II Army field cap and a shredded Brooklyn Dodgers tee-shirt; a moldy blanket covered his lap. After a week or two, I realized that the blanket hid the fact that the man had no legs, and that's when I started depositing a dime into his cup. He would tip his cap, but he never seemed capable of saying anything—he would just smile, revealing a broad expanse of toothless black gums. By the time each day's deliveries were finished, he was gone, and I always wondered how he got on the plank each day, where he went at night, and—of course—what had happened to his legs: Was he born without them? Could anyone even be born without legs? Did he get run over by a subway train? Had he fought for the United States in the War and had them blown off? I guess that's also when I started to realize that some questions are never answered.

On those sunrise walks, I came to believe that Brooklyn's shops and tall buildings and tenements and brownstones actually expanded in the growing light of day not as buildings that had been carefully planned and constructed, but as nature's outcroppings, reminding me of pictures of mountains and caves and boulders in distant places like Montana and Wyoming and California, places I had seen in books and magazines… places I assumed existed but had never observed myself and doubted that I ever would. And when I saw lights flicker on in some of the buildings, I thought that maybe the stars had moved inside to help the people who lived there start their day.

Sally-Boy was always at the bakery a couple of minutes before I arrived, probably because I took so much time to develop each morning's mysteries inside my head. We would fill our wagons, get our delivery list from Angelina or Massimo, and laugh and punch and wrestle our way through our delivery route. And Sally had been right—every day, a few people would give us a tip, an extra dime each or sometimes even a shiny quarter. When our deliveries were completed, we would return to the bakery, hand over our checked-off delivery lists, and help out as needed. By early afternoon, we would be on Sally-Boy's fire escape, counting our money and discussing vividly what we would do with it:

"We can't see the Dodgers any more, but we can go see the Yankees if you want," I said.

"I will always hate the Yankees, and I hate the Dodgers because they left us!" Sally said angrily. "I might go see the Yankees just to boo them all game. Hey, maybe we could take the subway down to the ferry terminal and take the Staten Island ferry across the water and see what the hell is on that island. They say the ferry is free to ride! Can you believe that?"

"Yeah, I heard that, too," I said. "We can do all of that."

"And even more stuff," he said, lowering his voice, though it was just the two of us on the fire escape, "like maybe we could buy somethin special for Angelina and surprise her."

I laughed but saw he was serious. "Like what?" I asked. "What would we buy her?"

"I don't know," he said. "I don't know what to buy girls."

"She's not a girl. She's all grown-up."

"But she's nice like a girl, right? I mean, she's always nice."

"Uh oh," I said.

"What?"

"You are in love with Angelina, Sally-Boy!"

"Shut up! I ain't in love! She loves Massimo. I just want to do somethin nice for her."

"Because you are in love with her!"

"Shut up!"

He banged the railing for emphasis, but I could not stop teasing him, and soon we were having our usual fun wrestling and spitting at each other on the fire escape.

Sally-Boy never mentioned buying Angelina a present again. But we did go to see the Yankees play a couple of times, and Sally booed so much the fans around us told him to shut-up, and we went to Coney Island—but not to the mysterious Staten Island—with my parents and played games and rode rides using our own money... and around the neighborhood, we got to be known by the moniker on our tee-shirts: "Bakery Delivery Men." People would call out to us, "Hey, Bakery Delivery Men, bring me a coupla more tiramisu tomorrow, eh? You know where I live." My Mom laughed every time we were greeted that way, saying, "Look how well you have done, Mikey! You and Sally-Boy are the most famous kids in the neighborhood." She would look at my father for agreement, but he would just say something like, "It's very good, Anna…for now," and he would gently squeeze my shoulders.

About a week before the summer ended, just a few days before school was about to start, Sally and I completed perhaps our biggest delivery and then sat on the fire escape counting our money. "I don't want school to start," Sally said.

"I don't either," I said.

Sally stood and spat over the railing. "Let's not go."

I walked over next to him and looked down at the street. "I wish we didn't have to," I said.

"Why do we *have* to?" he asked.

"Because…well, that's what we have to do. We have to go to school. We have to learn stuff."

"What stuff?"

"I don't know. Like math and stuff. And about mountains and planets and other countries."

Sally shook his head as he looked at me. "You're stupid," he said.

"Shut up! Why do you say that?"

"School is stupid, and if you want to go to school, you must be stupid."

"You *will* be stupid if you *don't* go to school, Sally, and you know it."

Sally looked at me with relaxed eyes. "Yeah," he said, "maybe. But I liked this summer. It has been a good summer, and it's almost over. Look at the money. We made that money."

"We'll do it again next summer," I said.

"Promise?" he said.

"Cross my heart and hope to..."

"Don't say the rest of that!" he interrupted quickly, grabbing my shoulder hard. "No, don't you say that last part, Mikey!"

"Okay, okay, Sally," I said, and he relaxed his grip. "I'll just cross my heart that we'll do it again."

"Me and you," he said, "we are The Delivery Men."

Sally stared straight ahead over the railing at something, but I could only see the brick and asphalt and concrete that together formed Brooklyn's familiar buildings and streets, streets we had walked every day that summer, streets that led to the bakery, to the people, to the fire escape...to our homes.

EPISODE #6

HARRY

I knew I had another cousin—a guy named Harry, who lived somewhere in Connecticut—but I had never met him. All I knew about him was that he was ten years older than I, and he was the son of my father's brother, Thomas Burns, a Seaman who had been killed on a ship during World War II. Harry lived with his mother and a man who was now his father, a relationship I had trouble understanding—in my eleven-year-old mind, "stepfather" and "stepmother" were words filled with evil connotations. Sally-Boy and I even philosophized deeply on the topic while stretched out on the fire escape the day before we started sixth grade. Harry, his mother, and stepfather were passing through Brooklyn briefly to see us on their way to dropping Harry off at some college called, I thought, University "in" Maryland:

Me: "If you have a father, then that's your father, right? I mean, having a stepfather, that's not like having a real father."

Sally-Boy: "Yeah, your father is your father. Someone else can't just say that he's your father. It gets bad when they do that. Papa tells me that someday I might have a 'stepmother,' but that would never be like having a real, actual mother…like you have."

Me: "Your Papa tells you that? That you might have a stepmother someday? I wonder where she would come from."

Sally-Boy: "I dunno, but maybe she will give me money just to be good…or try to smack me around! Does your cousin Harry's stepfather give him money? Is he nice?"

Me: "Who knows? I've never met Harry or his stepfather or his mother. Harry goes to some college in Maryland. That's one of the states."

Sally-Boy: "I know Maryland is a state! I'm not that stupid, you dummy! Harry must be smart if he's going to college. I'm never going."

Me: "You don't know that."

Sally-Boy: "Why? You really think you'll go to college? You want to do all that reading and studying? For what?"

Me: "I don't know. Probably not…but maybe."

Sally-Boy: "I bet Harry's stepfather is making him go. That's what they do. And that probably makes Harry mean. That's what happens when you get a stepfather or stepmother; you get mean because they make you mean."

Me: "Well, they are all stopping by the bakery today, so I guess we will find out."

Sally-Boy: "Yeah, well, I'm gonna keep an eye on that stepfather."

Me: "Probably a good idea, yeah."

A little later that day, when Sally-Boy and I arrived at the bakery, everyone was already there—Harry, his stepfather, his mother, my parents, and Uncle Sal were laughing and enjoying their coffee and sweet treats. My father spotted us first, and he said, "Look who's here, Harry! My boy, Michael, and his cousin, Salvatore. You guys, it's about time you met Harry!"

Harry stood up from behind the small wooden table, and his body just seemed to continue stretching. Eager to shake hands, he smiled and extended a long arm toward us as we approached. I gripped his hand, and he said, "It is so great to meet you, cousin! I have been waiting for this for a long time."

"Nice to meet you," I muttered, slightly overwhelmed by his height and the fact that he was wearing what Sally-Boy and I and the other kids at school referred to as a "sissy golfer's shirt," a short-sleeve pullover with blue-and-yellow checks and an open collar.

Harry turned to Sally-Boy and said, "And you must be Salvatore, Junior—or Sally-Boy, if it's okay for me to call you that."

"Yeah, sure," Sally-Boy said, putting his hands in his pockets rather than shaking Harry's. "You can call me that. I don't care."

My father then introduced us to Harry's mother, whom he referred to as, "Your Aunt Gloria," and then to Harry's stepfather, "Your Uncle John." My Aunt Gloria waved to us both and said, "Hi, fellas," with a nice, but quick, smile, and Uncle John nodded and said, "Nice to meet you guys. We were wondering if you were going to show up. Where were you?"

I was caught by his slightly accusatory tone, so I hesitated, which gave Sally a chance to jump in: "We was out bustin windows," he said calmly. "That's what we do."

Big Sal immediately said, "Why would you say that, Salvatore? What's wrong with you?"

But Harry started to laugh loudly at Sally-Boy's comment, and said, "Hey, that sounds like fun, guys! If I had more time, I'd come bust some with you! Maybe we could punch someone's lights out, too, know what I mean?"

Aunt Gloria said, "Harry! That is not funny. Don't give these boys any more ideas!"

"Mom, Sally-Boy was kidding," Harry said. "Take it easy. No one was breaking windows, right, fellas?"

"Right," I said. "We were just sitting on the fire escape, talking like we do and then it got late. That's all."

"Now that really does sound like fun," Harry said. "Taking it easy on a fire escape on a warm day. I like that."

"Well," Harry's stepfather said, "I guess that is as good a way as any to spend a day here. But we have to finish up our coffees and get ready to continue our drive to Maryland."

Harry turned to his stepfather and said, "We have a little more time. I'd like to talk with these guys some more."

Uncle Sal said, "Let me get the coffees freshened up, and that'll give Harry a few minutes to talk with these knuckleheads. Okay?" Harry's mother and stepfather looked at one another quickly and then nodded reluctant approval.

"Let's talk outside," Harry said. "Come on. We need some privacy. After all, we have to figure out which windows to break next, right?"

As we walked out of the bakery, Harry's stepfather said, "Not funny, Harry! And remember—we leave in ten minutes."

The three of us sat at one of the small wooden tables under the awning in front of the *Panificio di Boccanera,* an aria wafting softly from inside the restaurant. "Do you guys get to hang out here a lot?" Harry asked. He looked relaxed as he leaned back in his chair and stretched his long legs.

"Yeah, pretty much," I said. "We both work here, too."

"Nice!" he said. "This is a great spot. And you get to do some work here, too. Great!"

"What's so 'great' about it?" Sally asked.

Harry looked at him and smiled. "Because, it's so real," he said. "You have lots of people to talk to and buildings all around you and everyone seems to know everyone. And the bakery seems like a beautiful place to work—the coffee, the pastries, the opera."

"You mean you don't have places like this where you live?" I asked.

Harry laughed. "In Connecticut? No, the town I live in is not like this at all. Don't get me wrong; it's very pretty. Nice houses, a great college called Yale is nearby. The beach isn't too far…"

Sally interrupted him: "Well, we got colleges, too, and Coney Island and Jones Beach and others not so far away."

"Yeah, oh, I know that," Harry said calmly. "I'm not saying one is better than the other. But this is just nice in a different way from what I am used to. You might find Connecticut nice in a different way, too."

"I got no interest in going there…to Connicut," Sally said, adding his own pronunciation.

"How about you, Mikey?" Harry asked. "Think you'd like to visit someday?"

"I guess," I said. Sally-Boy turned and looked at me sharply, and I continued, "But I don't know enough about it. Maybe. I don't know. I like it fine here with

Sally and the bakery and working and the fire escape and our friends."

Harry nodded. "Sure, I understand, trust me," he said. "It's good here. Where is this fire escape where you guys hang out?"

Sally looked down the street in the opposite direction of his apartment building. I explained to Harry that the fire escape was a few blocks away on the seventh floor of the building where Sally-Boy lived.

"Sounds very cool," Harry said. "I don't have time to visit it right now, but I would like to see it someday and talk with you guys while we sit together. Would that be okay?"

Before I could say, "Yes," Sally-Boy blurted out, "Why? Why would you wanna sit on the fire escape with us? You got your own home in Connicut and you got your own beaches and you got your own college. It's just a fire escape. Our fire escape."

"Oh, hey, I get it," Harry said. "I didn't mean anything. I just have always wanted to meet you guys, and now that I have, I'd like to get to know you more. It's cool to have cousins."

"I ain't your cousin," Sally-Boy said. "Mikey is, but I ain't."

"Yeah, well, I hear you guys are like brothers, so the way I look at it, we're related, we're family. But it's no big deal, Sally-Boy, and I didn't mean to piss you off at all.

Look, I just like you guys, and it's great finally meeting you, so I hope we will stay in touch somehow."

Sally stood. "I gotta take a piss," he said. He shoved his chair aside and walked into the bakery.

"I like Sally-Boy," Harry said. "Tough kid, but I can tell he's a nice kid, too. He loves his neighborhood. And this is a great bakery his dad has."

"Yeah," I said. "Everyone likes the *Panificio*. Does your father—I mean, stepfather—own something?"

"No, he teaches in a private school. Classic literature."

"I don't know that... 'classic literature.'"

Harry laughed. "It's interesting stuff, great to read, makes your brain grow."

"And you're studying it in college, right?"

"No, no, I study business. Someday I plan to own my own business."

"You can study how to make a business? Like a bakery?"

"Oh yeah, you can study all about business in college, but probably not a bakery for me," he said, chuckling. "I do want to do something nice, something fun, make someplace where people can go to enjoy themselves. This bakery is a good model, but I'm no baker. I'm still figuring things out. Hey, maybe we'll all work together someday—you, me, Sally-Boy. You never know." He stood up and said, "I better go take a pee myself before we take off."

I got up to walk in with him and reached up, grabbing his shoulder. "Hey, Harry," I said, "is your stepfather nice?"

"Sure," he said. "Why?"

"I don't know," I said. "I mean, he's not your father, right?"

"Well, no, not biologically, Mikey..." he paused, seeing my confusion at the word, and then went on, "in other words, John wasn't my mother's first husband. I don't remember much about my real father. But John is good to me and to my Mom. He's taking me to college and helping me pay for it. He's a good man." He gave me a gentle punch on the shoulder, and added, "Not all stepfathers or stepmothers are mean, you know."

Just then, Sally-Boy and the others emerged from the bakery. "Running in to use the bathroom real quick, Pop," Harry said to Uncle John. "I'll be right out."

There was a lot of hugging and hand shaking and promises to visit again soon. When Harry came back out, his parents were waiting in their car for him. He got into the car and called out to me and Sally-Boy, "I'll see you guys again sometime! It was great meeting you! Now go bust up some windows!" They drove off, and my parents started walking home, holding hands. Uncle Sal, Sally-Boy, and I walked back into the bakery.

"Harry said his stepfather is nice," I said to Sally. "He said Uncle John is helping pay for college, and he's a teacher. But Harry wants to do some sort of business someday. He says…"

Sally cut me off, stopped walking, and faced me. His eyes quickly scanned my face, and his jaw protruded. "You and me, we're cousins," he said. "You ain't ever seen Harry before, and he's all talking like you are his cousin and like I'm his best friend…maybe even brothers like you and me are. But he ain't. And his father ain't your uncle, really. He's like a…a step-uncle. Your real uncle is dead. Just like my Mama. Mama was your real aunt, but she's dead. My Papa is your real uncle. And I am your real cousin. Your brother." He paused, started to walk away, and then turned back to face me again and added, "Not Harry."

A short time later, I walked home. My parents were sitting outside on the stoop of our small home, talking with a couple of neighbors sitting on their stoop next door. As I walked up, my father said, "So, Michael, what did you think of your cousin Harry? Pretty impressive young man, right?"

"I guess so," I said. "He seemed nice."

"Was there something you didn't like about him, honey?" my mother asked. "He certainly seemed to like you and Salvatore."

"And," my father added, "he's on his way to finishing up college at the University of Maryland. My brother would be very proud of him."

"He said he likes his stepfather," I said, "and he wants to make a business someday where people can go and have fun. He said maybe Sally and I could work with him. And he wants to visit the fire escape sometime to hang out with me and Sally-Boy."

"Would you like that, Mikey?" my mother asked. "Would you and Sally like to have your big cousin join you on the fire escape someday and talk with you about stuff like that?"

I thought about it and pictured three of us, not just two, on the fire escape. I imagined Harry there—tall, educated, talking perhaps about a new business—and suddenly the familiar, comfortable fire escape image grew increasingly blurry in my mind. Seeing it that way made me uneasy and, at the same time, I started thinking about questions I might have for Harry: What is college like? How do you get in? What do you study when you say you study 'business'? How do you do that? Why did you go away to college when you could go to that one you mentioned that was close to home—"Yell," I think it was called? Then my mother said again, "Mikey? What do you think? Would you like to have Harry visit sometime and sit with you and Salvatore on the fire escape?"

"I don't think so, Mom," I said.

"Why not?" my father asked sharply.

"Well, it's, it's where Sally-Boy and I go."

My father whispered something to my mother that I just barely heard: "This is what I mean, Anna!"

He quickly looked away from her, and she just gently touched his arm. Then she said to me, "Just think about Harry, Mikey," she said. "Someday you may want to talk with him a little. That's all, honey."

I nodded, and I could once again see the fire escape clearly in my mind. "Yeah, Mom, maybe," I said. "But probably not on the fire escape."

EPISODE #7

FIVE BUCKS

O ur role as "delivery men" provided us with unexpected status and recognition in the neighborhood, something Sally-Boy and I did not fully realize until we started sixth grade at St. Anne's Elementary. We had become neighborhood figureheads, celebrities of sorts, and from the very first days of school that year, our classmates treated us differently. Sure, some comments were typical smart aleck remarks like, "Deliver this!" (Monte Grafenski's favorite, as he grabbed his crotch, though he always followed it with a laugh just to be sure he hadn't made us angry—he was clearly afraid he might wind up face down in the dirt again) or "I got a tip for ya right here!" (blurted out by several guys and, of course, also followed by the obligatory crotch grab).

Most of the kids, however, wanted to know details about how much money we made, how long we had to work, and how they might get a similarly "cool" job at the bakery next summer. And we especially welcomed the uniformly positive comments from girls: "I always liked it when you came by our place," said Gina Falengina, the prettiest and nicest girl in the class. Her friends Patsy Sullivan, who was taller than most boys in the class, said, "Yeah, those tee-shirts you wore were neat!" and Austina Petrucci, the math whiz of the class, admitted, "I almost came to the door in my pajamas one morning to say hello to you but Momma said, 'No!' I mean, I was covered and everything, but I just wanted to say, 'Hi.'" Lots of giggling ensued, and Sally-Boy and I would try to control our blushing as we exchanged confused, yet knowing, looks with one another.

Exactly *what* we knew was uncertain, but the fact that we were now different certainly was clear, although Uncle Sal said during the school year, we would only make deliveries on weekends. The newfound status carried over to the bakery in the afternoons, when we would dutifully report for other work inside Uncle Sal's shop. In those after-school hours, there were always small groups of men, many of whom had been "investors" in the *Panificio*, crammed around the small wooden tables, playing cards or checkers, drinking their coffees, attempting to sing along with the opera, and filling the shop with smoke, boisterous laughter, and conversation that ranged from ear-splitting volume to grim-faced whispering. Invariably, they greeted us with shouts of "The Delivery Men are here! *Qui sono i principi!*" and sometimes they would even stand and bow when we entered as though we actually *were* princes.

One rainy spring afternoon shortly after our birthday, Sally-Boy and I approached the bakery and saw the shades drawn tight and the neon sign turned off—signals that a "meeting" was taking place inside and that no one else was allowed to enter. But Sally, who during the summer had begun peppering almost everything he said with various profanities, said, "Shit, we ain't standin in the rain waitin for them to open the damn place. We're goin in."

"Think we should?" I asked. "We've been told to stay out when the shades are down. Maybe it won't be too long."

"Our asses are gonna be soaked," he said. "It's my Papa's shop. Let's go." Sally reached into his book bag for his emergency key and we entered through the front door, tossing our book bags into a corner. In unison, six heads turned toward us, and all talking stopped, except for one stern voice.

"Hey, Delivery Boys, what the hell you think you're doin? Yous ain't allowed in here wit the shades down! You know that." The speaker was a man known to me only as "One-Eyed Jimmy," a guy who wore a perpetual smile, but the cross-shaped scar where his right eye should have been was the dominant feature of his face. His left eye was surrounded by thick lashes and an eyebrow so bushy his eyeball was scarcely visible.

"It's rainin out so we came in, Jimmy, but we are goin to go into the kitchen right now," Sally-Boy said.

"But yous ain't supposed to come in at all, right?" One-Eyed Jimmy said.

"Yes, but..." Sally started to say as I grabbed his arm and began pulling him toward the kitchen door behind the service counter.

"Stop!" Jimmy ordered. Sally and I froze. Jimmy stood and slowly walked toward us, flicking ashes onto the floor along the way. Directly in front of us, his eye suddenly seemed like a powerful needle that could control not only our movements but also our thoughts. "You two guys think yous can do whatever you wanna do, eh?" Jimmy said. Then he turned to the other men at the table, who sat smoking their cigarillos and blunts, and asked, "Whaddya think a these guys, eh? They come in, they interrupt us, they disobey our rules. We should teach them a lesson, right?"

"Yeah, a lesson they won't forget," one of the men said casually. He blew a smoke ring and added, "Maybe we should oughtta cut their balls off."

All of the men laughed at that remark, and Sally and I started to change our route, retreating slowly toward the front door, but Jimmy grabbed us.

"We'll go back outside," I said.

"Yeah," Sally said. "It's not rainin that hard now."

"Nah, nah, nah, nah," One-Eyed Jimmy said, his lone eye scrutinizing us with increasingly penetrating detail. "You came in, yous broke the rules, now you don't get to just back out like nuttin happened, you unnerstan? Now sit down." With one foot, he kicked two chairs toward the table where all the men sat.

Sally and I sat as ordered. Maybe it was my imagination, but I thought I felt us move closer to one another at that point, so close that it seemed we could have sat in one chair together. I wiped moisture from my forehead with my forearm. Sally stroked his upper lip. Was it rain from our walk? Or sweat from the bubble of fear swelling inside us? I was pretty sure I knew the answer.

"So," Jimmy said after he settled back into his chair, "you guys got some balls, eh? That is, unless we cut them off, right?" All of the men around the table laughed, grunted, or coughed. "But if we was not to cut your balls off, maybe you could use them to do a little somethin for us. Waddya think, eh?"

"Sure," I said right away, trying to remember the kind of coffee and pastry Jimmy liked, figuring he was going to ask us to grab some items from the kitchen for him. "What can we get for you?"

"'*Get*' for me? You mean like from the kitchen? Kid, I can '*get*' whatever I want whenever I want from the kitchen. I don't need *you* to *get* nothin for *me* from the kitchen."

"Then what do you want us to do?" Sally asked.

Jimmy looked at Sally, then turned to the other men around the table. "This kid," he said, swatting Sally gently in the head, "this one wants to know 'what.' Can you believe that? We got him by the balls, while he still has balls, and he wants to know 'what.'" Again, laughter, grunting, coughing. Jimmy turned back and looked at Sally. "It don't matter *what*, kid. You want your balls, you use them to do what we tell you. Sometimes, you don't have no choice. You should just say that you'll be happy to do whatever I want you to do, eh?" He blew smoke in Sally-Boy's face.

Sally didn't even move to brush away the smoke. He just nodded.

"Good. So now we unnderstan one another. Me and the boys here, we got a little delivery we need made. Yous are The Delivery Men, right? So yous can help us out, keep your balls, and maybe make a little something extra for yourselves. *Capisci?*"

Despite Jimmy's tone, I started to relax, wondering what kind of baked goods he wanted us to deliver, because I knew he didn't *deliver* stuff even though he could *get* whatever he wanted from the kitchen…and *where* he'd want it delivered …and whether he would let us wait until the rain stopped completely. I also realized a peculiar, persistent tingling sensation in my scrotum.

With a simple cupped-hand gesture from Jimmy, a man sitting across from him produced a fat envelope and slid it across the table. "I like it, Jimmy," the man said, nodding at us. "Ain't no one gonna stop these kids, these Delivery Men. I like it." The others around the table blurted out various sounds of agreement.

Jimmy picked up the envelope and held it directly in front of our faces. "See this envelope?" Jimmy asked.

Sally and I each assured him that we could see it.

"Good," Jimmy said. "Very simple. You gotta take it to a place on Myrtle Avenue. I'm gonna write down the address on the envelope. You got half an hour to get it there. Yous deliver it on time, yous come back here, I give yous each five bucks, then yous forget about it."

Sally and I looked at one another. Then Sally said, "You'll give us each five bucks just for delivering this envelope?"

"That's right," Jimmy said, leaning back in his chair. "I mean, who can't use five bucks, right?"

"Yeah," one of the men called out, as Sally-Boy and I stood to leave, "anyone can use five bucks...plus, you get to keep your balls!" Another eruption of laughter, grunts, and coughs filled the room as Sally and I walked into the pouring rain.

We were soaked by the time we got to the address One-Eyed Jimmy had written on the envelope. We knocked on the door of the brownstone, but no one answered.

"What do we do if no one's home, Sally? We can't leave it, can we?"

"Hell no," Sally said, "unless you don't want your balls anymore!" He grabbed his crotch and we both forced an uncomfortable chuckle.

I banged on the door this time, and we suddenly heard a man shout, "Comin, goddammit, quit beatin on the fuckin door for crissake!" But when the door opened, a black-haired woman in a tight black skirt and low-cut red blouse stood holding a cigarette. She looked startled to see us at first, but then she smiled at each of us and shouted to someone inside the house, "They got kids bringin the envelope, Gino! What the hell they thinkin?" She paused and looked at us from head to foot a couple of times and then said, "At least they're cute kids, these two."

"Who gives a shit about who it is or how 'cute' they are, goddamit! Grab the goddam envelope, shut the door on 'em, and don't use my fuckin name again for crissake!"

"Gimme the envelope, boys," she said, sighing.

Sally handed it to her. We started to walk away.

"Wait," she said. We turned to face her. "How old are you anyway?"

"Twelve," Sally said. He seemed to push his chest out, so I did the same.

She blew smoke out of the side of her mouth. "Twelve, eh?" she said. "Kinda big, ain't ya? Look strong, too. You guys strong?"

We both nodded, afraid to look directly at her since her breasts seemed to be growing out of her blouse as she spoke.

"You twins or somethin?" she asked.

Sally and I shook our heads simultaneously.

"Well, you should be," she said. "Hey, gimme your names. I might have some work for you sometime. Make us all a little extra money."

We told her our names, and I started to give her my address, but she stopped me just as Sally elbowed me slightly.

"I won't remember all of that," she said, "but I'll remember 'Salvatore' and 'Michael', and that's all I need to know when I have some work for you. I'll find you; count on it. But you didn't hear this, or nothing else, from me...not any of it, okay?"

"Okay," we said together.

"Go now. Get outta here. And remember, cuties, you were never here and you didn't hear no one's name. Got it?"

We nodded, as though mesmerized.

"See ya soon, cuties," she said with a wink and slammed the door in our faces.

When we returned to the bakery, the shades were back up, the neon sign was on, and it had stopped raining. My father had arrived early either from one of his jobs or from one of the college courses he was taking, and he was sipping coffee and talking with Uncle Sal, Massimo, and Angelina. When he saw me, he said, "There you are, Michael! Where were you and Sally-Boy in that bad rain? Just playing around in the puddles? You're soaked."

"We ran an errand," I said.

Immediately, Uncle Sal looked at Sally-Boy and asked, "For who? Who did you run this errand for, Salvatore?"

"One-eyed Jimmy," Sally said. "He told us he'd give us five dollars each if we delivered somethin for him."

"Delivery from the bakery, like some tiramisu or some cannoli, right?" my father asked. I could tell from the change in his tone that he already knew the answer.

"No, Dad," I said. "It was just an envelope that he asked us to take to Myrtle Avenue for him."

My father, Uncle Sal, and the Bortuzzis all looked at one another, frowning and shaking their heads.

"This is it, Sal," my father said, sounding oddly exhausted, yet somehow still firm and definite. "They've gone too far. This is it."

"Kev, I know, but relax, I can handle it. I can talk to Jimmy and his boys. This ain't gonna happen again."

"It's not your fault, Sal," my father said. "It's just what I have been telling Anna. It's here, it's what happens, it's what these kids learn. It's Brooklyn, Sal, it's Brooklyn now, and it's only a matter of time…" He turned to me and said, "Grab your stuff, Michael. Let's go before it starts to rain again."

"But what about the five dollars One-Eyed Jimmy promised?" I asked.

With that, Massimo Bortuzzi, dug into his pocket and pulled out two five-dollar bills. He handed one to me and one to Sally. "Jimmy told me to pay you. He said to remind you what he always says, 'Who can't use five bucks?'"

"Uh uh, no, no," my father said firmly, pushing against Massimo's hand. "No. Put it away, Mass. Michael's not going to take that money."

"But, Dad," I said, "we made the delivery!"

Uncle Sal motioned for Massimo to put both bills back into his pocket, saying, "Salvatore isn't taking it either."

"Not fair, goddammit!" Sally shouted. "We made that fair and square. It's our money!"

"Salvatore, you curse again, and you won't go out to play for a week, you got me?"

Sally just kicked at the table and muttered, "It… just…ain't…fair!"

Uncle Sal looked at my father and said, "I am so sorry, Kev. Like I said, it won't happen again. One-Eyed Jimmy, you know, I known him since we was kids, since before they poked his eye out, and he give me some money to help open this place. So, you know how it is. But he'll listen to me. Trust me."

"I trust you, Sal," my father said, as he motioned for me to get my book bag from the corner. "I have known Jimmy since we were all kids, too, but he's not the same now. He's not. Brooklyn's not." He gently grabbed Uncle Sal's shoulders, and I could just hear his words as I picked up my book bag. "Believe me, Sal, Mass, Angelina. It's not about any of you. You are good people, and I want the best for you. It's about me and what I want for me, for Michael, for Anna. It's my *family*, I'm talking about."

As I picked up my book bag and walked back toward my father, he and Uncle Sal embraced. Massimo and Angelina watched, but their faces suddenly looked like an invisible vice was slowly squeezing their handsome features tightly together. Sally-Boy sat in a chair next to them and stared at the wall.

"Fire escape later?" I asked as I sat next to him.

"No," Sally said, standing almost as soon as I sat.

"Then what do you want to do?" I stood and looked into his eyes. They seemed smaller, narrower, like something I had seen before but not on him.

"I want to get my five bucks, maybe today, maybe another day, but I'm *gonna* get my five bucks," he whispered. "I could use five bucks, and I am going to get it."

"How?" I asked softly.

Sally-Boy's eyes seemed to shrink even more, and he said, "Jobs. I'm gonna do jobs for people. People who pay."

I looked at him staring ahead with his shrinking eyes, and I searched his face, desperately trying to see myself.

EPISODE #8

OPPORTUNITY

My parents were having another soft-spoken, high-ly animated conversation in the small living area just off the kitchen. I sat at the kitchen table, struggling with my math homework, which consisted of some mystery about graphs and independent versus dependent systems and intersections and other stuff that made my mind wander to the eternal mystery about why the Dodgers left Brooklyn—something Sally-Boy had reacted to by taking a Duke Snider baseball card, angrily ripping it into tiny pieces, and then flinging the pieces from the fire escape, screaming a long stream of creative obscenities at them as they floated into oblivion.

The tiny brownstone we called home was rented from an enigmatic little man whose name was Mr. Bigelow. I never knew his first name, and he was mostly referred to simply as "Mr. Big," the contrast between his physical stature and his name making him even more mysterious...and memorable. In the brownstone, the small rooms allowed me to eavesdrop easily on my parents' discussions. That's how I pieced together little bits of information about the Burns and DeRosa families, various details about our financial situation (which always seemed strained in discussion but comfortable enough for me in reality), and comments about something my father only referred to in whispers as his "future plan." But on that evening, as I wrestled with the logic of graphs and my confusion about the Dodgers, I heard phrases and intonation that struck me as different:

My father saying with unusual passion, "It's our chance, Anna. We will start a new life. I can hardly believe it!" And my mother responding, "Oh, Kev, you are so good and you want so much for us. I can't imagine it, but I am ready if you are." And him saying, "I am, Anna, I am so ready. It will be so good for us and for Michael. To get him out of Brooklyn; to get *us* out of Brooklyn. Such an opportunity, Anna!"

I know now that what I heard that night was my father articulating the realization of his well-earned vision. After returning home to Brooklyn from World War II, he received his bachelor's degree from City College, the result of seven years of grueling part-time study. He worked at a print shop during the day and as an attendant in Madison Square Garden most nights, fitting in his college courses whenever he could. My mother was a seamstress in a huge factory filled with what seemed like countless rows of sewing machines that hummed almost musically together. Neither of my parents had lived anywhere other than Brooklyn. But my father would frequently talk about the many places he wanted to see: Ireland, Boston, Los Angeles, and—most often—Washington, DC, which he always liked to remind me "is our Nation's Capital, Michael. It is the root of everything the country stands for, what I helped fight for in the War. Someday we will visit and see the White House, the actual Capitol building, and all of the memorials, and you will see how important and beautiful it all is!"

As I continued to draw random graphs, I suddenly realized my parents had stopped talking. I looked up to see them standing and hugging one another and walking in my direction. "Michael, Mom and I want to talk with you," my father said.

Immediately, my mind started running through recent events at school—grades seemed fine, no trouble lately. My interactions with Sally-Boy—well, there were the paper airplanes we launched from the fire escape with firecrackers attached, but no one was home at the time and none of the neighbors had seemed to notice. My work at the bakery—on time, Uncle Sal seemed happy, and though I did sneak longer and longer peeks at Angelina every day, eagerly waiting for her to lean forward so I could see her long black hair dangle in front of her blouse-covered breasts, I thought I had kept that subtle. "What, Dad?" I finally asked, as he and my mother sat down at the kitchen table with me.

"Daddy has some very exciting news," my mother said, looking first at him with great admiration and then at me with her head tilted slightly sideways and her lips trying to decide if they wanted to broaden into a smile or turn down sympathetically.

"Okay," I said. "What happened?"

"Well, Michael," my father said, "what would you think if I told you that we were going to Washington, DC? But not just to visit. To live!"

I thought about his words for a moment, trying to interpret their meaning—"going to Washington, DC," had certainly been one of his goals and one that interested me increasingly, but then he had added, with enthusiasm, "To live!" I could not imagine what that meant or how that could even happen. So I said, "Well, going there would be fun, I guess, but, but we *live* here. In Brooklyn. This is our home, right?"

"Well, it is now," he said, "and it has been for all of my life, and for Mom's, and for yours. But sometimes, Michael, things change. You get a chance to do something different, something you've always wanted to do, something that can make life better for everyone."

"Washington, DC, would be better for everyone?" I asked, wondering how anything could be better than the life I had at that time and then remembering how bad the baseball team in Washington—the Washington Senators—was. "Their baseball team stinks."

My father chuckled and said, "Yes, it will be better for everyone—for all of us. And you're right, their baseball team is not that good, but we will all enjoy going to Griffith Stadium, the ballpark in Washington, you'll see. And remember, the Dodgers moved out of Brooklyn, too, just like we're doing." He smiled, and added, "Washington, that city, that whole area, will all be so new and so exciting and filled with so many opportunities for us all."

I thought for a moment, trying to picture what he meant, what he referred to as "better," but I could not come up with anything. "Well, we already all work here, Dad," I said. "You already have two jobs and Mom works at the factory and I work with Sally and Big Sal. We already have all that. And maybe we don't have the Dodgers or Giants any more, but we still have the Yankees...or do you think they'll move someday, too?"

My father rubbed the top of my head, and my mother reached out for my hand, engulfing mine with her warm fingers, and said, "Daddy has a new job, Michael. It's one that he has wanted for a long time. It's a job that not many people can have. It is special, just like he is. And it's a job that will make our lives better."

I shook my head slightly from side-to-side as I looked back and forth at the two of them. They were strong people without being forceful. My mother had a way of dealing with everyone and every situation in a manner that seemed to generate happiness and made people want to be with her and to believe in her. My father had more visible strength, always appearing muscular in his tee-shirts and always specific and definite in his comments and decisions. He could look at me and provide an immediate analysis of what I had done or what I intended to do or what I needed to do. At this moment, my mother was making me feel a sense of acceptance of the news, and my father was making me know that it was going to happen—this was not a discussion as much as it was an announcement of our new direction. I suddenly understood it all—her warmth, his strength, and my role.

"When will this happen?" I asked, trying to sound strong, but then the real questions rolled out. "Are we leaving tomorrow? Will I get to finish sixth grade here—I mean, I'm almost done—and can I say good-bye to Sally-Boy and Uncle Sal or will we just...just leave?" My voice grew increasingly loud and it shook slightly.

"Michael, Michael," my father said, "of course you will finish the school year, and you will have plenty of time with Salvatore and Big Sal. We'll move late in June and even after we've settled into our new home, you will have lots of opportunities to visit Salvatore here, and he can come to our new house anytime. You'll see, son—you'll see."

"A house?" I asked. "Of our own?"

"Yes," my mother said, "our very own house, Michael. Daddy is going to Washington next week to pick it out. He'll take some pictures so we can see it."

"Okay," I said, but the information had reached the point of being overwhelming, so I said, "I think I'd better keep doing my homework now."

"Sure, honey," my mother said.

"It's going to be great, Michael, you'll see," my father said. "Opportunity, son. That's what gives people a chance in life. Opportunity! And this is a big one."

"Okay, Dad," I said. "I gotta, you know..." I pointed to my math book.

My mother leaned over and kissed my forehead. I couldn't look up. I heard my father move his chair back, and out of the corner of my eye, I saw him stand and somehow appear taller and stronger than ever. Then I blurted out, looking up at him, "What is the job, Dad? What is it...the..." I groped for the word that I don't know if I had ever used before..."the 'opportunity'?"

He straightened himself to his full height, smiled his sideways grin, and said, "Believe it or not, Michael, but your father is going to be part of the Secret Service in Washington, DC. Me, Michael! Kevin Burns. I'm getting out of Brooklyn and moving my family to the Nation's Capital."

"Oh, okay," I said, looking at the two of them holding one another and smiling down at me. I nodded, gazed intensely at my homework, and pointed my pencil meaningfully, as though I might actually be able to decipher the puzzling graphs. But as my parents retreated back to the room off the kitchen, I wondered if there were any fire escapes in Washington, DC, and what was secret about the Secret Service, and why people and baseball teams felt they had to move...and how I could ever tell Sally-Boy that I might have to root for a team like the Washington Senators.

NEW SKY

My father and I crammed the last of countless boxes containing our brownstone belongings into our newly purchased, but very used, Ford station wagon, and the three men in sleeveless tee-shirts from Lorenzo's Moving Service climbed into their dusty truck containing our furniture. The sun was just coming up behind the only home I had known for all of the twelve years of my life at that point. The street was quiet, though not far in the distance, the familiar sounds of a Brooklyn day dawning swelled up steadily—the hissing of truck brakes, the blasts of horns, the occasional shout in English or Italian or some language I had not yet become familiar with.

"Time to hop into the station wagon, Michael, so we can start our trip," my father said, an unusual degree of softness in his voice. "Washington, DC, is waiting for the Burnses to arrive."

I stood there, looking at the old stone house, the one sandwiched between the Cohens on one side and the Gionfriddos on the other. My mother exited our home for the last time, made sure the door was locked, and then blew a kiss to the now empty house before walking down the steps to meet us. She hugged me and my father simultaneously, and together we scanned the long row of brownstones that lined the block, all with almost identical chafing paint around their entrances and a similar pattern of cracked concrete on their four-step stoops that led to the sidewalk. We knew everyone who lived in them—people who hung out on the stoops nightly in tattered clothing and shouted to one another for any reason imaginable: to share food, to celebrate a Dodgers victory, to curse the Dodgers' departure, to toast a couple of newlyweds, to express sympathy for a recent death. At one corner was "Moishe's Candy Store," where Moishe Cohen, our neighbor, worked day and night and always gave me free candy and where my parents sent me to buy half a dozen fresh bagels every Sunday morning after Mass.

I looked at what I had assumed would be a permanent scene for my life and tried to imagine the new world that my father had told us about—we would live in "our very own actual house," as he referred to it, in a place called Virginia close to the Nation's Capital, and he would work in that still mysterious-sounding thing, the Secret Service. I did not understand the enthusiasm he expressed for his vague new job and for what he called "our new life"...all I could do was wonder what would happen to the brownstone, the people, the noise...and to try to imagine what my father had described repeatedly, always with a passion I had rarely seen in him:

"We are going to have our own actual house with a real big yard, Michael, where you can play baseball or football with your new friends. You won't have to play in the streets, and you will love all of the trees in the neighborhood—trees you can climb or build forts in with the other kids. And it's so quiet, Michael, you can sleep with the windows open without hearing anything other than maybe a bird or a cricket. And you can always see the sky because there won't be any skyscrapers or tenements to block it." He had shown me a black-and-white photograph of the house, but to me, it looked like pictures of old abandoned cabins and fading forests that I had seen in history books.

"But what happens here in Brooklyn?" I asked the night before the moving van pulled up in front of the brownstone. "What happens to our house here and to all these people and to my friends and to the trucks that we count going up and down the street?"

"They'll all still be here," he said. "They will all go on without us just the same as they do now. But where we are going will be less crowded, more open, with so many great new places for you to explore, and…"

"Yes, Dad, I know…'opportunities.'"

Still, although we had repeated the conversation several times, I stood there getting ready to climb into the station wagon and could not stop wondering what would become of "the neighborhood," as everyone on our block simply referred to it, and how wherever we were going could possibly replace it. So I stared at the brownstone, I scanned the street, I looked all the way down to "Moishe's Candy Store," and then I felt my mother's gentle hand on my shoulder.

"Time to go, Mikey," she said, bending over and kissing my cheek. "You'll see; this will be a wonderful adventure for us all, for our family. You'll see, honey."

I nodded, but I could not move even as she lightly tugged at my shoulder, even as I heard my father close the driver's side door and start the station wagon. I stood still as the men from Lorenzo's shouted to us and their moving van pulled away, grunting its way to the end of the block, leaving us behind.

"Let's go, kiddo," my father called from the car window. "We need to beat the traffic if we can."

But I just stood there, looking at what would soon be my past and wondering about what would be my future. "Give him just another minute, Kev," my mother said to my father. "We'll be right there."

She turned to me, and squatted so she could look directly into my eyes. "He's going to be okay, you know, honey," she said.

I said, "He will be, won't he, Mom?"

"Yes, honey, of course." She hugged me.

Into her shoulder, I said, "And I'll get to see him again, won't I?"

"Of course, you will," she said. "You and Sally-Boy both say you are like brothers, and you are. You are brothers, so you will always be there for one another. We will be up here to visit a lot—for holidays, and just think, in the summer, you can come up here and stay with him for a couple of weeks, and he can stay with us for a couple of weeks."

She let her arms relax, and I nodded again. "Okay then," I said. "I'm ready. Sally-Boy will be all right, and I'll see him again on the fire escape."

She took my hand, walked me to the station wagon packed with boxes that contained life as I had known it, and closed the door behind me. When she got into the car, my father said, "Everything okay now, Michael?"

"Yes, Dad, everything is okay."

"Just one thing, Kev," my mother said to my father. "Swing by once more for him."

My father tilted his head sideways and looked at her. "It's out of the way, Anna," he said.

"It's just a few blocks, Kev," she said. "Just let him take one more look."

"We'll be back to visit in a few weeks…"

"Kev, come on, let him have just a quick look."

Instead of heading down the street in the direction the moving van had gone, my father said, "Okay, if it means that much," and turned the station wagon in the opposite direction. I knew the route by heart, and I rolled down my window as we slowly pulled up in front of Uncle Sal's *Panificio di Boccanera*. The neon light flickered on in the window, indicating that the shop was just opening for the day. Uncle Sal was in the doorway with his back to the street, singing along with an aria that softly flowed from inside the bakery, so my father blew the horn and slowed the car to a stop.

Big Sal jumped but laughed and said as he walked toward our car, "*Maronna mia*! Whaddya doin, Kevin, you crazy Mick? You scared the *pipi* outta me! I thought you was outta here by now."

"Just thought we'd say good-bye…again," my father said.

"We'll see you again soon, Sal," my mother said. She leaned out the window, and Big Sal kissed her on the forehead.

"You *better* see us again soon…and *often!*" he said. "We miss yous already, for cryin out loud." Then Uncle Sal turned to me, reached into the car through the rolled-down window, and gently tapped the side of my head with his open hand. "And what about you, Mikey? I need your help in the store, knucklehead—you and my nutty son. You gotta come back to work, you hear me? I need you here. Sally needs you here."

"Sure, Uncle Sal," I said. "I will. Don't worry. I'll be back to help you."

"Gotta go, Sal," my father said, moving the car ahead slowly. "Trying to beat the traffic if we can."

"One minute," Uncle Sal said. He ran into the bakery and quickly emerged with a bag. "Here you go," he said, handing me the bag. "A few cannoli to nibble on during the long trip, eh?"

"Thank you, Uncle Sal," I said, taking the bag from him. My mother blew him a kiss, and my father said, "So long, Sal" as he pulled away.

"*Arrivederci!*" Big Sal called to us. I watched him disappear, waving to us the whole time.

As my father drove down the street, I saw my parents look at one another, and although no words were spoken, my father nodded, smiled, and mouthed, "I know."

Five blocks later, we were slowly driving past the seven-floor apartment where Uncle Sal and Sally-Boy lived.

"We can't stop, Mikey," my mother said, "but take a good look at it. It is going to be there for you whenever you want it. And he will be there, too."

"Sally-Boy," I said emphatically. "He'll be there, too."

"Yes," my parents said simultaneously.

We rode slowly past the old building that stretched crookedly into the morning sky, which was an early-summer blue that I saw clearly despite huge buildings nearby, and I craned my neck, counting the floors to the seventh. Then I spotted it, a little blurry from the distance—our fire escape off of Sally-Boy's apartment. In my mind's eye, I saw Sally-Boy standing on the familiar iron grate, waving. He had been angry when I had told him a month earlier that I would be moving. He had leaned on the fire escape railing, smoking and squinting into Brooklyn's jagged distance, listening to me without speaking, as I tried to explain as best I could in adult terms what was happening and why. I kept repeating statements like, "See, my Dad says I will be up here in Brooklyn a lot, and you can come visit us in Virginia as often as you like. There will be lots of fun things to do there; we'll be near Washington, the Nation's Capital, and we can explore new things and find new opportunities." Finally, Sally turned to me, took a long drag from his cigarette, and said as he exhaled a small cloud of smoke, "What the hell does that even mean, 'new opportunities,' Mikey? You believe that shit? Well, I don't; I don't buy any of that shit. It's just that your Dad, he thinks he's better than us and that you're better than us...that maybe you're like that guy Harry. But to me, to me, all it really means, Mikey, is that you're going away, probably for good no matter what shit you tell me, no matter how many times in the future we might sit on our fire escape...you're going away for good. That's just what happens. That's just the way things work." He flicked his cigarette over the railing and abruptly climbed back into the apartment.

Sally-Boy and I saw each other almost every day after that until the morning I left Brooklyn, but he always seemed preoccupied, looking around distractedly during our limited conversations on the fire escape, and rarely talking at length with me about anything...even when the bakery got broken into early one morning and the thief pulled a gun on Massimo Bortuzzi but Angelina saved her husband by sneaking out of the bathroom and breaking a wooden chair over the gunman's head. Normally, we would have spent hours on the fire escape dramatically retelling the incident, reenacting it, swapping glamorous images of beautiful Angelina raising the chair and slamming it over the gun-toting stranger's skull, while screaming curses at him in Italian. But Sally-Boy was right—things were different now, even when we were together in our safe space.

As my father drove on, I continued to stare at the speck that was our fire escape until the building slowly disappeared as though being absorbed into the sky. I reached my hand out the window and said so softly that even my parents couldn't hear, "So long, Sally-Boy." Then I put on my Brooklyn Dodgers baseball cap, slumped into the back seat, and pulled a cannoli from the bag. I took a few bites and felt myself falling asleep. I fought it at first, but eventually I allowed myself to drift off, glimpsing the Brooklyn sky above me, the delicious, familiar taste of cannoli filling my mouth.

ABOUT CHUCK CASCIO

A native of Brooklyn, NY, Chuck Cascio moved to the Washington, DC, area at an early age, but he remains a New Yorker at heart. Chuck, an award-winning journalist, educator, short-story writer, and business leader, is the author of three nonfiction books who has had hundreds of news stories, feature articles, and opinion pieces published in a wide-range of newspapers, magazines, and journals. *The Fire Escape Stories, Volume I*, marks Chuck's current focus on developing fiction.

Chuck earned a BS degree in Economics and Business from Wagner College on Staten Island, NY, and an MA in Communications from the American University in Washington, DC, where he later became an adjunct faculty member. Chuck also taught high school and served as faculty advisor to student newspaper publications in Fairfax County, VA, receiving extensive recognition for his innovative approaches to teaching. After leaving the classroom, Chuck served as Vice President for the National Board for Professional Teaching Standards and then as Vice President for Educational Testing Service.

Chuck and his wife, Faye (an award-winning science educator), are dedicated gym rats, who live in Reston, VA, near Washington, DC. You can find out about all of Chuck's latest works at **www.chuckcascioauthor.com**, and you can reach him at

chuckwrites@yahoo.com.

Made in the USA
Middletown, DE
29 March 2019